Whispers in Wonderland

Shannon Rose

Copyright © 2025 by Shannon Rose

All rights reserved.

No part of this book may be reproduced, distributed, or transmitted in any form or by any means, including photocopying, recording, or other electronic or mechanical methods, without the prior written permission of the author, except in the case of brief quotations used in reviews or critical articles.

This is a work of fiction and inspiration. Names, characters, places, and events are products of the author's imagination or are used fictitiously. Any resemblance to actual persons, living or dead, or actual events is purely coincidental.

For permission requests, please contact: shannonrosee93@gmail.com

Cover art and illustrations by Shannon Rose

Edited and designed by Shannon Rose

ISBN (paperback) 979-8-218-87324-0

First Edition: December 2025

Shannon Rose Publishing

For my mom, thank you for always believing in me.

Once upon a time, there was a rose, uncurling and unfurling each velvet petal revealing a sweet little fairy in the middle of the rose's blossom, and it was as if the fairy was blooming too! As the fairy fluttered her wings and smiled her first smile to the world, she could hear a whisper, and it was the universe that spoke straight to her heart.

"You are magic!"

the universe told the fairy

"Listen for the whispers in wonderland, for they shall *guide* you..."

and so, the fairy began a grand adventure, being guided every step of the way to her happily ever after, and these are her whispers in wonderland...

The Fireflies

"Be you in all you do, and the magic will always shine through."

The fireflies told the fairy.

"but, what can I do to be me... more?" The fairy asked

"Nothing, my sweet! Stop trying, just be!"

"Thank you, fireflies!,

There's no one else

I'd rather be than

me!"

The fairy said as she flew into
the forest with her heart all aglow

The Swan

"Oh, how I wish to be beautiful," The fairy whispered.

"My darling," the swan cooed, You are the epitome of beauty, for the magic of your heart shines through your skin.

Your magic is love...

and oh my heavens from above,

you are so beautiful,

so beautiful!"

"Oh, my swan!"

The fairy declared.

I will fall in love with myself more and more each day, for that is when my beauty can shine in every way. I will forever treasure the beauty of me. Now, I can see!

Thank you, beautiful swan!

The Caterpillar

"Remember who you are, my lovely..."
The caterpillar spoke.

You are more than you realize....
Remember who you are and you will
see all the love you bring, for you
make the world sing!

you are love, this is who you are,

and you are transforming into the
most beautiful you thus far!

"I remember who I am!"

I am love!

I am, I am!"

The sweet fairy said in her very own wonderland

The Tortoise

"Go slow, my sweetness."
The tortoise gently spoke to the fairy. "Mingle with the moment and linger a little longer.

The magic awakens when you slow down...."

"Thank you tortoise!"

The fairy exclaimed.

I will move a little slower and linger a little longer, even when my wings begin to flutter off in a hurry, I will take a deep breath, let go of the worry, and melt into the moment, for there is no need to scurry!

The Goose

"Loosen up and have some fun my dear," the goose reminded the fairy, "don't take everything so serious... instead,

twirl,

dance,

and

sing!

Let it go and let your feathers

flow!

This is the way to magic,

you know!"

I love being a

silly goose!

The fairy replied with a giggle.

The Chamomile Flowers

"Relax, my sweetness...
enjoy your beingness."

The chamomile flowers
told the fairy.

"Slow down &

savor

your adventure."

"Thank you chamomile!"

"I will savor the beauty, I will savor the music, I will savor my every sip of tea, I will savor every moment of this magical adventure of being me!" the fairy promised, as she sat on a cloud and gazed upon the beauty of her land.

The Mushrooms

"Listen to your body."
The mushroom said to the fairy.

the soft voice,
the loving whispers
from inside,
listen for its
Rhythm
it will never ever
speak a lie.

flow with

it's every movement

dance &

flow!

and treasure your
beautiful body
as you move & glow!

The fairy wrapped her arms around her body in a snug little hug, as she said, "I embrace my body's wisdom, and I will fall in love with every inch of me, and beauty is all I shall see! I honor my body as a sacred temple, a beautiful home for me."

"Thank you mushroom!"

The Elephant

"Stay true to your heart, you have always been magic from the very start!"

The elephant told the fairy.

"Stay *true* to *you!*"

"Thank you sweet elephant!

I will always stay true to myself and to my heart. I will listen to the magic of my heart, for it is my true compass, that shall never part. My love is my magic, it is my art! I will always stay true to me!"

the fairy replied as she skipped through the forest. She felt love grow in her heart more and more, and she realized love was the key that opened every magical door.

The Honey Bee

"Bee happy, my *honey!*"
The honey bee said.

"Bee love"
bee enchanted
by the flowers,
and by the *beauty*
all around and above!

and most importantly,

live your life unconditionally

love unconditionally

& simply

bee."

"Thank you for sharing your sweetness with me!"

The fairy replied,

"Beauty is now all I can see and I shall love unconditionally. I will give from my heart with no expectations, for nothing more than because it brings me joy. And I will be happy because I choose to be. I love being me!

Thank you, honey bee!"

The Sparkling Stream

"The secret my dear is, *flowing not forcing,* the sparkling stream in the sunlit meadow informed the fairy

"Just let it flow,

soft & slow

let the rules go

and simply know,

you are love and

you glow!"

The fairy felt her wings begin to calm down to a gentle flutter, she felt her thoughts relax, until there was not even a mutter, her gaze began to soften as she melted into the moment, like butter. "Oh thank you, sweet stream!" The fairy allowed herself to simply flow, just like the stream in the meadow, it was a gentle kind of magic that didn't show, for it was more than you can see, it is the magic that just is. She let every resistance go and let herself flow.

The Birds

"Listen for the beauty all around you today."

The birds softly chirped to the fairy.

"Let this sweet, sweet symphony play!

What can you hear far, far away?

What can you hear up close today?

And listen closely to what others have to say... Simply listen to the magic whisper and *sway*."

"Thank you beautiful birds!"
The fairy told the birds.

"I will listen closely to the magic all around, to every gentle sound, for there is so much music to be found!"

The Fairy Godmother

"Flow to the magic of inspiration!" The fairy godmother told the fairy. "These are the whispers from the universe sent straight to your heart!"

From these inspirations
you create art!

after all, my lovely
you have been an
inspiration
from the very start,
you are a work of
art!"

"Thank you. Thank you. Thank you, Fairy Godmother!"

The fairy shouted with glee! "I love the magic of inspiration, and I love the artwork of me! I will follow and flow with everything that fills my heart with wonder, inspiration, and curiousity, for that is when my magical creations shall begin! I love being inspired and I love to create, and I love love love that I am a creation from God's inspiration!"

The Cat

"Let your confidence shine!
You are
beautiful, sacred,
and divine!"

The cat told the fairy.

"Pounce and play and take little naps along your day Just remember you are

purrfect

in every way!"

"Thank you sweet kitty!"

The fairy replied, as she felt her purrfect self come into light.

"I will let my confidence shine as I light up every forest I walk into — My every step is sacred and I will believe in myself meow and meow." The fairy coughed to clear her throat, "Oops, I think I meant more and more, but meow fits, doesn't it?" The fairy giggled as she pet the cat's fur and she could hear the cat purr and purr and purr.

The Fairy's Mom

"Never, never, never

give up, my darling!"

The fairy's mom said.

"Do not believe in those who say, "you can't" when your heart says,

"I can"

Believe in yourself, for you are

magic!"

The fairy could feel the magic within her heart begin to cheer, and without any fear — a grand surge of confidence appeared and the fairy knew from this moment forward, she would never give up on what her heart held dear.

"Thank you mom! I love, I love, I love you!"

The fairy replied with a heart full of love. It felt as if, "I love you" was not nearly enough, for this love was infinite, a kind of love only a mother and daughter could understand.

The Frog

"Trust in the magic, my sweet."

The frog informed the fairy.

"Let it  you

off your feet!

Trust, allow love,

and repeat!"

"I think you mean, Ribbit!" the fairy replied as she began to rephrase his words.

"Trust, allow love, and ribbit!" The frog pondered the fairy's comment for a moment, as he squinted his eyes in great consideration, and finally he answered, "I do suppose I meant both, Trust, allow love, ribbit, and repeat! I love to ribbit, and it's very important, indeed!" The frog chuckled and began to ribbit, ribbit, ribbit, and of course, repeat his ribbit some more.

"Thank you frog!"

The fairy smiled upon her new, singing friend, as she thanked him with divine gratitude, "I will trust in the magic. The magic that is all around me, even when I cannot see, for that is the beauty, and I will allow love to always flow, and I will ribbit my own kind of fairy ribbit as I go, but of course, that you already know. And every time I hear your frog song echo through my ears,

I will trust in the magic, the magic always guiding me. The magic right here!" The fairy touched her heart with the palm of her hand and began to flutter her wings to her next destination.

The Sunflower

"You are **perfect** as you are." The sunflower said.

"Stand tall in your **enoughness**

because, you

illuminate

the

world!"

"Thank you sunflower!"

The fairy answered, as she felt herself shimmer & shine.

"Confidence shall be one of my superpowers, thank you sweet sunflower! When I believe in myself, my whole world shines too, and only love shall shower. Thank you for sharing your magic from up there in your sunshine tower!"

The Rose

"Open your heart,

my lovely."

The rose whispered to the fairy.

"You are *love*

it's time you let yourself receive!"

"Thank you, beautiful rose!"

The fairy replied, with a
heart full of love

"I will keep my heart open to all
the whispers of love, because love
is a gift, for which, I have an
infinite supply of!"

"You are a *treasure,* you are a gift from god."

The pirate announced to the fairy.

"Take pleasure in the treasure you are and watch your treasure chest **overflow!** Never forget how valuable you are, for you are **the bounty,** my sweet!"

"Oh, thank you Pirate!"

The fairy replied, as she felt her own worthiness shine.

"I will forever treasure the magic of me! My smile is a treasure, my body is a treasure, my talents are a treasure, and my love is a treasure that I cannot measure. Thank you for reminding me to not search for my treasure chest, but to remember it is within."

The Dragon

"There is no need to fear, whenever you are scared, I will protect you."

The dragon told the fairy.

"You are made of *magic* you are *love,* sweet one."

"and I *love* you." The fairy whispered.

The Chameleon

"Relax, little one..."
The chameleon told the fairy.

"Relax into your body and feel your every color glow!"

"You are one of a kind, it's time to let your every uniqueness show!"

"Thank you, Chameleon!"

The fairy began thinking of everything that made her different from everyone else, and instead of beating herself up for being different and ever so unique, she felt each uniqueness glow from within her like the most gorgeous glowing colors. She realized they were nothing to criticize herself about, but instead they are gifts!

"I am magic, I am one of a kind!" the fairy declared as she celebrated her own beauty and magic.

The Ladybug

"You are lady *love!*"
The lady bug declared to the fairy.

"Love yourself with all of your heart, and that is when the magic starts!"

"Oh, thank you, lady bug!"

The fairy replied and gave this little bug a gentle hug.

"I choose to honor myself, to respect myself, nourish myself, praise myself, and love love love myself everyday! I choose to love myself today!"

The fairy fluttered her wings, and as she flew away, she could feel the energy of love sweep her off her feet in the most beautiful way.

The Daisy

"Notice all the beauty around you today, and your garden shall bloom in every beautiful way!"

"Thank you, beautiful daisy!"

The fairy exclaimed.

I will go on a treasure hunt every day to discover beautiful things. I will notice the beauty in every moment, the beauty in others, and the beauty in myself. I will focus on these beautiful treasures, and savor such pleasures..."

The Fish

"Allow your every ocean wave to flow..."

The fish told the fairy.

"You know exactly where to go." the **magic** is in the journey, Just flow...."

"Thank you fish!"
The fairy replied.

"I choose the way of flow, to let go, and trust my waves to flow, flow flow! There is nothing I need to figure out, because the flow already knows where to go. I will sit back and enjoy the magic in every moment upon my journey — that is my flow, to let go and trust and know I am always guided exactly where I am meant to go!"

The Hummingbird

"Thank you sweet hummingbird!" replied the fairy.

"I love following the flowers, I could do it for hours and hours, I am so full of love for that is my power, and I shall treat myself every single day to something sweet, and I will give sweetness to everyone I meet!"

The Oak Tree

"Be one with the trees,"

The oak tree whispered to the fairy.

"Ground your roots into the Earth, be still, and listen for the whispers in the wind. They shall always send you in the perfect direction. The wisdom is always here, listen..."

"Thank you, oak!"

The fairy declared, as love infused the air, and this is what she began to share,

"I am grounded and I am calm, like the trees, and I dance with the breeze — always flowing. And I will always listen for the birds and the bees, and I will listen even deeper, I will listen to the magic in the wind, and the magic within."

The Autumn Leaves

"Be wild and free!
Let your expectations
fly into
the
breeze."
The leaves told
the fairy.

"You do not
need to hold on
to a thing."

"It is even more *magical* than it seems...

Let go and fall in *love!*"

"Thank you, Autumn leaves!"

The fairy replied.

"I am letting go of every need to control, and instead I fly with the breeze, I open myself to love and ease!"

The Mouse

"Simplify, my darling..."
The mouse told the fairy.

"Let it be easy,
let it be fun!"

"Choose the way of flow,
go slow, and simplify as
you go."

"Thank you, sweet mouse!"

The fairy said, rather simply, but with gratitude that overflowed.

"I let it be simple and fun. I let go of being perfect, I let go of everything complicated, I let go, I let go, I let go! Oh, how I love to simply flow!"

The Prince

"You are enough."
The prince told the fairy.
"exactly as you are,
there is nothing you
need to do to prove your
enoughness, you have
come so far.

just be as you are,

for you, my sweet, are enough."

"Thank you, my sweet prince."

The fairy could feel love shine from her heart as if starlight was sparkling within her. The fairy opened her mouth, hoping to find the perfect words to express her gratitude and her love for the prince, yet no words came out. Instead, she gazed at him, not only with her eyes but with her heart, and they both knew there were no words to be spoken, for the fairy, her prince, and this love was more than enough.

The Unicorn

"Give yourself time to rest."
The unicorn told the fairy.

"Beauty sleep is simply the best!"

"Thank you, unicorn!"

The fairy yawned a little yawn, as she felt her wings relax upon her back. "Silly me!" The fairy exclaimed, "From all the magic and exciting things, I almost forgot to relax!" The fairy cuddled up upon a cloud and flew away into her own little dreamland, as she stopped worrying about what to do next and allowed herself to simply rest.

The Sloth

"Plus, the s l o w e r you go, the more time you have to enjoy your *adventure!*"

"Thank you, sloth!" The fairy replied with a heart full of gratitude.

"I choose to move slowly and with ease, finding flow in the slow within every moment. I will feel into my body and the magical energy of me. There is no need to rush through life. I will flutter my wings in this moment, enjoying and savoring my moment of now. Slowly, gracefully, and easily is how I fly and flow!"

The Grasshopper

"Every day in every way, fill your life with gratitude! Let it infuse your every mood!"

The grasshopper told the fairy.

"I'm so grateful for you, grasshopper!"

The fairy replied, as she leapt in the air, feeling ever so grateful for her legs that move her and for her wings that fly her and for this very moment that holds her.

"I choose gratitude!"

the fairy declared.

The Snowflake

"There's no need to control, sweet girl,"  the snowflake said.

"Begin to dance and **trust** your dance

for your every

move is guided

and

perfect

as it is!"

"I love to dance and flow, thank you snow!"

The fairy replied, as she twirled and danced with the delicate snow swirling all around her.

The Racoon

"You are a *masterpiece!*" the raccoon told the fairy. "Celebrate the beauty of you and every little magical thing you do!"

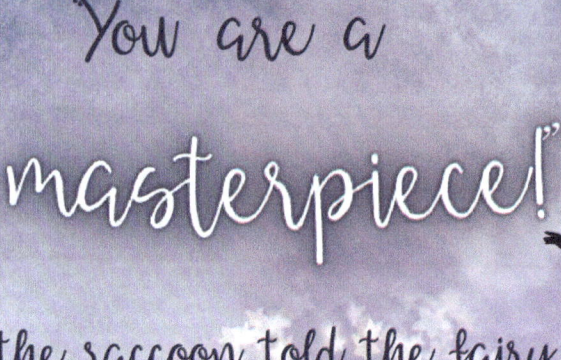

"Celebrate the **beautiful,** imperfectly perfect, divine, and one of a kind creation of you!"

"Thank you raccoon!"

The fairy smiled a sweet kind of smile, the kind of smile that can make you feel warm and cozy even on a cold, rainy day. A kind of smile that can make the grumpiest person begin to smile too. The fairy replied to the raccoon, as she smiled her sweet smile, "I will begin to celebrate each step I take, and I will give myself praise for every accomplishment I make, no matter how small. I celebrate the magic in everything I do and everything I create!"

The Owl

"Who am I, really?" the fairy asked the owl.

"You are the **who** you've been searching for all along!" the owl began.

"It is you,
take a
peek
you are everything
that you seek
its true! you
are
the who!"

"Oh, my feathers!"

The fairy shouted with such enthusiasm, she even surprised herself.

I am who I am! I am the who, who already is whole and complete.

The who has always been me!

Thank you Owl!"

The Rabbit

Make one small hop in the direction of your desire every day! and don't forget to play along the way."

"Thank you, Rabbit!

it just so happens,

I love to

hop!"

The fairy declared, as she bounced and skipped and hopped upon her trail.

The Snowman

"Create, create, create, and play!" the snowman exclaimed. "Let your passions lead the way. Create something beautiful today!"

"Thank you Snowman!" the fairy replied,

"I love being creative and I tap into my divine creativity with ease and grace, always knowing I am in the perfect time and place. I will feel into my inspirations and create from that loving space, for my every creative project is supported by the universe's magical embrace!"

The Stars

"Follow your light, my love," the stars told the fairy

"The whispers in the night the love that makes your heart take flight!"

Follow your light

look at you shine

so bright!

Oh my stars, you are such

a beautiful sight!

Just follow your light!

"Thank you shining stars for reminding me to follow my light. Silly me, I almost forgot about my light within, my inner compass which is never dim! Thank you, thank you, thank you!

The fairy thanked the stars as she danced upon the grass below, and the stars and the moon illuminated her path, and the fairy danced and giggled as she felt her own light shine brighter and brighter than ever before.

The sweet little fairy realized that her wings had become rather heavy and her eyelids just couldnt stay open much longer, as she was beginning to get rather tired upon her adventure. She decided to fly back to her cozy little home within the petals of a rose to rest up for a while. The fairy kept each whisper she received today within her heart, like little love letters she could always come back to. Before the fairy tucked herself in bed and closed her little eyes for the night, she gave thanks again to each whisper, feeling gratitude warm her heart like the coziest of blankets.

The fairy fell fast asleep with a sweet little smile upon her face, eager to awake in the morning and begin another day in wonderland, because that's the beautiful thing about beginning another day — a new adventure begins!

Thank you!

Thank you, thank you, thank you, my lovely reader!

I am so very happy you picked my book out of all the books to choose. My heart overflows with so much gratitude and love and I sure hope you can feel it! I have been in the process of writing this book for five years, and I can't help but smile, knowing someone else out there is reading it, and smiling too!

I also hope this book invited more magic into your life, and has inspired you.

Thank you for journeying upon this adventure with me and your new favorite fairy!

~ Shannon Rose

About the Author

Once upon a time, there was a girl who believed in magic, and she let that magic flow through her words.

Shannon Rose lives in a little cottage in Northern California, where she writes fairytales, poetry, creates art, and practices yoga. Her world is filled with love, flowers, and a whole lot of magic. Shannon hopes to inspire her readers to embrace their creativity, to follow their hearts, and always believe in magic.

If you'd like to stay up to date on her many magical adventures, follow her on Instagram: @shannonrosee_xo

Made in the USA
Coppell, TX
23 January 2026

69455355R00095